Melanites

The Origin

Written By: Tarreka Garnett   Illustrated By: Baba Aminu Mustapha

Dedicated to every magically melanated person who has forgotten the power they possess. As people of color, we must always remember that without us, this world is just an existence but with us; it lives.

About the Author

Tarreka Garnett, author of: *The Sleepover, Rising Phoenix- Controlling the Flames, Cooling the Embers, and Rising from the Ashes*, and *Melanites-The Origin,* was born and raised in Miami, Florida. After graduating from Florida A&M University, with a Bachelor of Science in Elementary Education, she went on to become an educator in Tampa, Florida. For the last 14 years she has dedicated her life to advocating for and educating students in high poverty areas of Hillsborough, County.

As an educator she noticed that of all the origin stories she's read to her students, there wasn't a story that told children about the melanin in their skin. Tarreka wrote Melanites-The Origin because she believed that it is important for children of color to know why they have melanin in their skin and to see the beauty of that melanin.

Long ago, on what is known today as the continent of Africa, was the land of Melania. Melania was the most beautiful place on the planet with vast grasslands and rainforests that were home to Earth's most majestic animals.

Lain beneath the land were rubies, sapphires, garnets, and diamonds nestled beside stones of gold and copper.

Every morning Mother Sun greeted Melania, and as the day forged on, she enjoyed watching the cheetahs sprint across the savannah and the crocodiles patrol the river ever so quietly. Of all her planets Mother Sun appreciated the beauty of the Earth the most, and as time went on her love for Melania grew stronger and stronger.

One morning as Mother Sun peeked over the Earth's horizon, she started to feel that Melania needed a leader to care for it. Mother Sun knew that without proper care, Melania would not evolve, and it would eventually perish.

So, as a gift to the planet that she loved so much, Mother Sun created a people of leaders who would care for Melania and the Earth.

Mother Sun wanted to create a people who would embody the beauty of the land and the power of the animals, while also having the intelligence and wisdom to invent and create new technology.

To give them strength and knowledge, Mother Sun harnessed the spirit of animals like the elephant and the eagle. For speed and agility, she channeled the spirits of the cats that protected the grasslands. To give them wisdom and fortitude, to withstand the test of time, she decided to place in them the essence of herself.

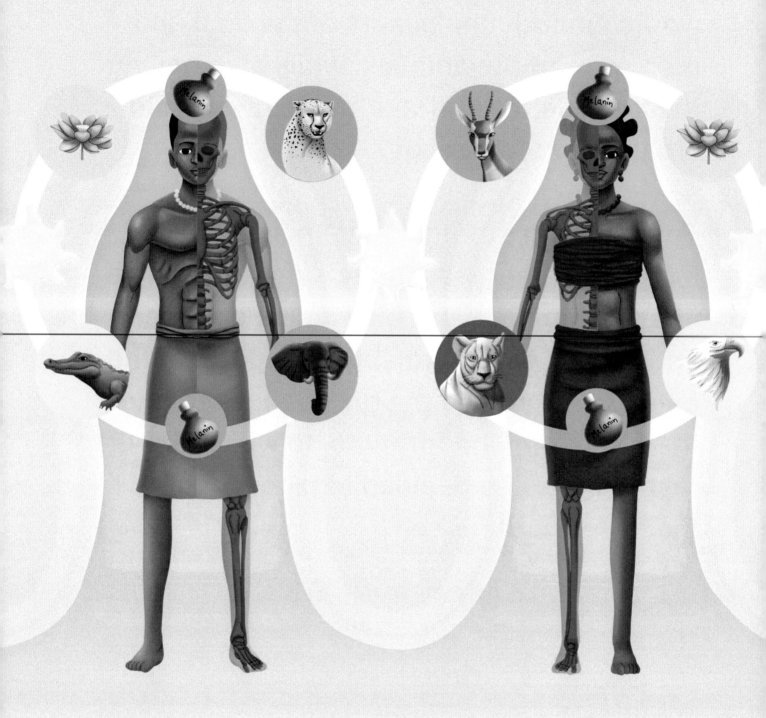

Designing the new leaders of Melania was one of Mother Sun's greatest accomplishments and she was very careful to ensure that they were in perfect balance with the Earth. But before she could finish, she realized that she needed to protect their bodies from her ultra-violet rays and extreme heat.

To protect them, Mother Sun placed a magical pigment, called melanin, in their skin. The melanin would help shield the new leaders of Earth from her rays and, more importantly, melanin would hold their magical powers.

Once Mother Sun was done, she placed the new leaders of Melania on Earth and decided to call them "Melanites".

It took seven days for the Melanites to awaken but one morning as Mother Sun lit the sky, she saw a group of people in varying shades of black and brown tending to the land. As their skin sparkled in the sunlight, they built houses, grew crops, and made Melania their home.

Mother Sun was extremely pleased to see them take control of the land, and she was confident that they would love Melania as much as she loved them.

As time moved on, the Melanites quickly grew wiser and more curious. One day as they worked, a young woman cried out, "We have done all that we can, what more can we do for Melania?"

To which a young man replied, "Look around at what we have been given. The land, water and air all belong to us. Without us this place is an existence, but with us; it lives! Our souls are forever connected to Melania, so we must take care of it. We must keep working and in time, the land will give us all we need."

One evening, as the Melanites prepared to retreat to their homes, they looked to the sky to find that Mother Sun was completely eclipsed by the moon. In an instant, every Melanite fell to the ground and into a deep sleep.

While they slept, Mother Sun placed magical powers in their melanin. These powers would give them the benefit of a forever youthful appearance and, if nourished and cared for properly, their powers would make them the most powerful people on Earth.

Once everyone had a power, the eclipse ended, and Mother sun dimly filled the sky with light again.

When the Melanites were reawakened
Mother Sun called to them:

"To every single Melanite
this land is yours it's true.
If you take good care of it
it will take good care of you.

In your skin there is power
it's in your melanin.
The magic it contains is great
though some will say it's sin.

Stand together, and be as one
for complete power you need each hue.
Although the land may separate
your melanin unites you.

Each day I rise I will be
the strength of which you need.
When things get tough, because they will
work together to succeed."

Feeling successful, Mother Sun began to retreat into the sky when she heard a small voice cry out, "Mother Sun! You have given us so much and for that we are grateful, but how will we ever repay you?" To which Mother Sun replied, "I only ask that you continue to evolve and pave the way for the generations after you. You are no longer the only people on Earth, and a great battle is near. This battle will change life as you know it, but you must always remember who you are the powers you hold."

And with that Mother Sun returned to the highest point in the sky and continued to shine her light on Melania.

After watching Mother Sun disappear behind the clouds, the Melanites stood for a moment and said in unison, "Our melanin holds our power!"

Just as the words drifted from their lips, power surged from their bodies. Some were lifted into the air, and they became the keepers of the wind. Some fell to their knees and when their fingertips touched the soil, it came to life. Other Melanites were drawn to the ocean, and they became guardians of the water. The rest of them eagerly watched as flames sprung from the palms of their hands. The Melanites were excited about their new powers and couldn't wait to learn how to use them.

But in their excitement, they forgot about the battle that was looming. And soon after they received their powers, Melania was invaded and the Melanites were faced with unimaginable terror.

The Melanites didn't know that they were being watched from miles away. The other people, who were now on Earth, became afraid that the Melanites would use their powers against them. These people decided to capture the Melanites in hopes of stealing their powers and, because the Melanites had yet to master their abilities, some were eventually captured and forced out of Melania.

Mother Sun watched in sadness and knowing that she couldn't intervene, she whispered to the Melanites:

"The time has come for you to know
that pain and strife is part of growth.
You must remember your power lies in
the magic of your melanin.
One thing for certain and two for sure
for pain and strife there is a cure.
Through it all work as one and not few
to take back your land, you will need each hue"

Being the only people who could hear Mother Sun, the Melanites vowed to secretly develop and grow their powers until they were reunited as one.

It took over 400 years, but the Melanites were freed, and legend has it that today Melanites are all around us. They look *normal* and have adapted to *normal* human life, but they can be recognized by the melanin in their skin. Their shades vary. Some have darker skin, and some have fairer skin but throughout the years, their melanin has continued to hold their powers.

It is believed that Mother Sun has been quietly waiting for the twenty-second year of the twenty first century to reignite the powers of the Melanites. And when this time comes, they will no longer be able to live as *normal* humans. The power of their melanin will force them back into greatness and together, they will become the most powerful people the Earth has ever seen.

Glossary

Africa- The second largest continent in the world. Africa lies between the Atlantic and Indian Oceans. It is in the Eastern Hemisphere.

Eclipse- The blocking from view of the sun, a moon, or a planet by another celestial body. In an eclipse of the sun, the sun is hidden from earth's view by the moon passing between the sun and the earth

Evolve- to develop, change, or improve by steps

Fortitude- strength, endurance, and patience in the face of adversity or temptation

Generation- the entire group of people who were born around the same time.

Hue - a particular color; shade

Surge- a rise, increase, or rush of something.

Technology- a field of knowledge having to do with the practical applications of science and industry, or the inventions and methods of solving problems that are produced through research in these areas

Unison- speaking all at the same time, or singing at the same time

Wisdom- good judgment and an understanding of that which is true or good, knowledge, learning

Activities

Word Search

E	D	U	T	I	T	I	T	R	O	F	G	N	T	F	Y
T	M	E	E	W	E	N	U	N	E	A	I	I	G
I	E	N	Y	E	I	V	A	N	G	T	E	U	O
A	R	I	H	E	E	S	O	A	I	T	N	E	L
R	I	A	E	V	U	G	D	L	A	S	T	N	O
A	N	E	E	G	R	U	S	O	V	T	O	I	N
A	A	I	N	A	L	E	M	E	M	E	R	N	II
F	N	G	A	E	A	I	T	U	O	E	E	F	C
R	I	H	G	E	N	E	R	A	T	I	O	N	E
I	I	U	L	A	T	T	E	N	R	A	G	U	T
C	A	E	T	I	N	A	L	E	M	E	A	A	N
A	T	G	E	E	M	C	E	C	L	I	P	S	E
T	T	U	E	C	T	H	T	A	R	R	E	K	A
M	O	T	H	E	R	S	U	N	R	G	L	N	A

EVOLVE	MELANIA	GENERATION	GARNETT	MOTHER SUN
SURGE	MELANITE	TECHNOLOGY	AFRICA	TARREKA
ECLIPSE	WISDOM	HUE	FORTITUDE	

Think Beyond the Text

Throughout the story you will notice that the Melanites are shown crossing their arms in front of their chests. This symbol was inspired by the way a Pharaoh (most important and powerful person in an Ancient Egyptian kingdom) was laid to rest and it also means "hug" in American Sign Language (ASL).

Why do you believe Mother Sun created the Melanites with their arms crossed on their chests? (Use details from the text to support your answer)

_____

_____

_____

_____

_____

_____

_____

Made in the USA
Columbia, SC
15 October 2022

69105874R00020